CAPSULE STORIES

Masthead

Natasha Lioe, Founder and Publisher
Carolina VonKampen, Publisher and Editor in Chief
BEE LB, Reader
Aimee Brooks, Reader
Stephanie Coley, Reader
Rhea Dhanbhoora, Reader
Hannah Fortna, Reader
Teya Hollier, Reader
Mel Lake, Reader
Kendra Nuttall, Reader
Rachel Skelton, Reader
Deanne Sleet, Reader
Annie Powell Stone, Reader
Claire Taylor, Reader
Emily Uduwana, Reader
Amy Wang, Reader

Cover art by Darius Serebrova
Book design by Carolina VonKampen

Paperback ISBN: 978-1-953958-14-3
Ebook ISBN: 978-1-953958-15-0

CAPSULE STORIES

Summer 2022 Edition

Swimming

Contents

Swimming

You go to the edge of the water and wade in, slowly at first. The waves lap at your toes, then your calves, then your thighs and hips and stomach until you give in and let the water carry you. The water gently cups your body, lifts you, and you feel weightless for the first time in years. The stress sinks away until it's just you and your body and the water.

You feel strong as your body pulls you smoothly through the water, farther from shore. You remember the games you used to play as a child, seeing how long you could hold your breath, diving for toys in the deep end, racing your cousins across the pool. Big breath in. And then you let yourself grow heavy, sink further and further from the surface until your feet hit the bottom. No one can see you down here. It's different underwater, quieter and smooth, everything muffled and distorted. You glide around, discovering a whole new world, until your lungs are screaming and you push off toward the surface to come up for air.

You float and float, the waves washing over your skin, the sun beating down, your mind on nothing at all, until at last it's time to go. You vow to come back again soon, to return to this feeling, to return to the water.

Madison Park, July

Betsy Sharp

City heat embeds us under glass
pressed and glued with sweat
between fluorescent slabs
until our lungs lie flaccid in surrender.

Now is when we place our trust in water:
offer bodies to be lifted
an act of simple faith
ourselves becoming liquid
slip fluently between the tongues of light
find relief in cool dissolving
move and slide and glint
on lapping overflows of green
till barriers of stuck flesh wash away
and throats begin to pulse with memory of fluted gills.

Mother Superior

Chelsie Kreitzman

I stand fidgeting on Sand Point Beach,
where the water is as clear as the forest-fed air.
Even in July, I wish the sand felt warmer
beneath my bare feet.

The grains seem coarser here than at Chapel Rock,
where I made Jack stop on our hike
to scamper barefoot down the dunes,
where we put our feet in the turquoise water
just so we could say we'd stepped in.
But our love affair with the lake has moved fast;
we crave more than the casual dipping in of toes.
We've vowed to completely submerge ourselves
in her frigid waters.

I volunteer to go first.
Jack watches me as I shift my weight,
hesitate.
"It's never going to get any easier," he prods,
so I do it the only way I can:
shrieking
as I run toward the water, as if that will help me
ignore the sharp-toothed cold
that bites my ankles, knees, thighs,
nearly makes me double over
when it reaches my torso.

Once the water's too deep to keep running,
I tuck my head and shoulders down fast,

like a child afraid of monsters
diving under a blanket at night.
Jack splashes in after me, laughing.
We swim, let our bodies grow pleasantly numb.

Later, he remarks that the water felt pure,
that he came out feeling cleaner
than he was before. I agree,
but I think the lake cleansed my soul, too,
sparked something inside me back to life
like a baptism by fire—
or ice, as it were—
a holy moment spent cradled
in the arms of Mother Superior.

completely
submerge
ourselves

Cradled

Eve Croskery

We had two weeks to wait—
two weeks to hide and hope
and hold our breath.

We head to the coast;
maybe the hum of the ocean,
swell of the waves,
sand underfoot,
will somehow calm our
racing hearts.

I float on my back in the lagoon.
Water cradles me, amniotic warm,
ears fill with muffled promise.

This body no longer
feels like my own.
Suspended in glassy waters,
I imagine our baby,
placed within me with surgical precision,
floating too in his watery world,
a tiny nautilus—spinning, spiraling,
coiled tight and snug.

The sun spilling onto my skin
feels too bright for this
to be anything but true.

Twenty-One Weeks

Eve Croskery

At the scan I watched
your heartbeat flickering rhythmically
on the screen, a tiny pulse of promise.

I let out a wisp of breath.

After, I swim, a celebration of sorts,
my belly swollen just enough to confirm
this is not a trick.

I cradle this life in my hands,
proudly, tentatively, protectively.
Salty droplets gather on my skin
and catch the light.

This joy feels perilous as I remember
all the days I drifted here
cold and empty
and could not fathom a time
when the sun would shine again.

Gold Dipped

Eve Croskery

Late afternoon light spills gold on our skin,
shadows long as I wade out past the breakers.

I hold her naked body, pink and shining
as the day she was born, while she wiggles

at the feel of the water's embrace,
mesmerized at the sight of it rippling,

glinting, reflecting. She grabs my face,
pulls it toward her, all soft dimpled hands and

wet open-mouthed kisses. Her eyes
hold oceans as she drinks the sun.

Last summer she floated here in my belly as I drifted,
swollen legs and aching back with the tide.

I clasp her rib cage, my hands outstretched
as she frog kicks and slaps the surface again and

again. Droplets fly and I feel the bom-bom
bom-bom of her heart—tiny and fierce—

beating so swiftly at the beauty of it all.

Always

Eve Croskery

He clings as the water holds us,
arms and legs knotted tightly.
He is caught somewhere
between the thrill and the fear of the sea,
he feels her power
as the swell lifts us and lowers us.

Sunlight paints shapes
on rippled sand beneath my feet.
He loosens his grip on my shoulders,
desperate to swim.

I watch him float
between his wonder at the waves
and the comfort of my arms,
between baby and boy,
between us and him.

When finally he finds the courage
to kick off from my mooring,
I realize he can only be brave
because he knows
I'm always here,
arms outstretched,
waiting.

When Grandparents Come to Visit

Eve Croskery

And for the first time this summer
I have the chance to swim, swim free,
submerge my entire body, dive and drift,
no child clinging to my arms.
Responsibility sheds from my skin.
I'd forgotten how to breathe.

Back on the shore, they play together,
digging moats, hands big and small,
pressing sand into fairy-tale castles.

I watch on, as if gazing
at a picture in sepia tones.
I drowned within our four walls,
the days blurred while
I slowly sank.
Now—I come up for air,
kick toward the mottled light,
water glints like broken glass.
I rise and fall with the receding tide.

Their laughter floats on the air
while I float on my back,
close my eyes, unclench my jaw,
feel the lapping in my ears,
the sun's hopeful warmth on my cheeks.
The water wraps herself around my weary bones.
I am weightless as worries wash off me
into the lukewarm salty sea,
for now at least.

Somewhere Upstate, I Watched My Child Find His Lungs

Belle Gearhart

The swimming hole is in the open palm of the woods. Off NY-212, down W Hurley-Zena Road for a quarter mile, it is only a breath away from downtown Woodstock. It is called Little Deep, and somewhere else there is a Big Deep. The air conditioner in the 1992 Acura is busted, and we keep re-adjusting our bodies, backs slick with sweat against the leather seats. The baby, pensive in his car seat, is a pale pink, his small forehead damp, curls sticking to skin. My partner turns where I tell him to, and we look ahead, into the crush of trees, where supposedly relief is waiting in a tepid silence.

No one is there at the swimming hole. It is a solitude I am grateful for. The swimming hole is a glorified creek, banks of dirt on either side of a current of cloudy water. Thin trees stand rigid, their branches coming together overhead to create a canopy. Large boulders are jammed into the gums of the bank, slate and dampened by water. The three of us stand still in reverence for the quiet; we are stereotypical city people, breathless in the wake of nature calls and the language of plants as they rub against each other in velvet breezes.

I strip off my T-shirt and step out of my shorts, clad in only a black bodysuit, because I have lived in the city for nearly a decade, devoid of public pools and uninfected ocean water, and have had no need to buy a bathing suit. My body is lumpy in the clingy bodysuit, fingerprints of pregnancy all over me. I feel my partner watching me; I am not shy under the kiss of summer, of heat, of humidity. Here is my body in all its motherness: uneven and textured, roadmaps of growth and then deflation on my hips.

I unclip the snaps of the baby's onesie and tug it over his head, and I see his small chest fall in a sigh of relief. He is a little over a year old now, his thighs chunky, and his hips are narrow like his dad's.

"We didn't bring a swim diaper," my partner reminds me, and I shrug, pull open the baby's diaper, the dip of his lower back swampy from sweat. My partner shakes his head, looks around, as if someone is going to burst from the trees and yell at us for allowing our small son to be nude in the gracious emptiness of the woods.

The water is brazenly cold, and the baby bursts into laughter as we take our first steps into the lake, as if we are walking into the world's funniest joke. The bottom is soggy, sandy, and I feel my feet sink as I put my weight forward. Up to his chest, he is squealing, alive, the swirling of water familiar, home again in some amniotic sac; I pull him against me and he is weightless, and I am an anchor once more.

"Take him," I call out to my partner, who stands on the edge of the water, shaking his head at the chill. I float the baby to him, swim backward, and feel the bottom of the lake suddenly disappear. I kick to keep myself up before diving under, and I want to scream in happiness, feel the cold in my lungs, open myself up to it. I swim to the other side of the lake and clumsily scramble up a rock, slimy with moss, and I feel my bodysuit ride up, my ass slipping out, exposed underneath the fibers of sunlight that fall through the branches above my head.

"Look at your mama," my partner whispers to the baby, who is looking disgruntled at the fact that his dad won't take him any deeper than ankle deep. His small hands reach out to me, and I slide back down the rock, into the water again, and I let my body go; I feel the extra baby weight from pregnancy hang off me, the plushness of my thighs floating in suspension, and I am suddenly twenty-one again, sculpted and carved and perfect.

When I resurface, he is waiting for me, open-mouthed and bouncing on small knees. I push away water in cupped hands, closer and closer, until my belly is touching the slope of the lake, that full belly once again, a scar couched in its softness. I am a snake, and he is screaming in joy, and I snatch his waist, his squirming body against me like a feral creature, wanting to dive headfirst into rebirth, in renewal. I watch my child learn about holy water; I watch our bodies relearn themselves in the runoff from a sacred mountain miles away.

I float on my back, and he is on my chest, looking at me with wild eyes and blue lips, as if to say: today is the first day I have known the world.

Slide

Ali Sharman

The dragon calls with a siren song
That ripples across the water's surface.
With pink plastic scales and grinning head,
Its curves beckon you, dare you,
To ride.

Halfway up the metal staircase your pace begins to falter.
We mountaineer higher together into cooler, thinner air,
And the radio-drone of your toddler chatter
Quiets as we summit,
Slowly, in line.

Your fingers search out mine as we conquer the peak of the
steps—
An umbilical joining of hands—
And, like this, we await our turn at the apex of the slide,
Out of the luxury of the sun,
With a shiver.

Three-year-old eyes fix on
The torrent of water
That cascades
Down the shadowed curve of the tube.
Down, down into the belly of the beast.

You nest in my lap at the water's edge,
Nails gripping thighs,
My legs pushed as wide as a laboring mother.
And off we push into the raging rapids
And we glide and we glide
And we fly—
Round corners
Round bends
A shriek of delight
(Yours or mine—who can tell?)
Arms reaching to the sky like a prayer
Of thanks
For each twist
And turn
And burst of slippery speed
Through the dragon's insides.

A moment of pure darkness—

Then mirrors of light from the surface below
Illuminate the final watery descent as
We are airborne—just for a second—
You and I.

We are weightless,
Limitless,
Two souls conjoined
In downward flight,
Birthed into the pool.

Hand in hand, we wade out from the dragon's mouth,
Bubbles of laughter in our throats.
You turn starstruck eyes up to mine,
And I already know what you will say—
Mama, can we do it again?

Freedom Is

Matthew Miller

Slinging a frisbee over Caribbean
waves, my six-year-old
circling the pool without
supervision. A swim belt
snapped beneath his arms.
That's the most important thing
to pack, more than floral suits
or Superman underwear.
A collaboration, one of us
smashes its foam to the bottom
of the suitcase and later we unwind
the belt's straps, clicking them together
across his timid heart.
My wife can leaf a magazine
while he splashes through shallow water,
testing trust on every step. At last,
he's ready for all the deep water.
My toes tighten on the beach.
He leaps off the side with uncertain
screams. Freedom is buoyant,
pulling him up from blurry shadows
to the surface, its rippling gleam.

A Six-Year-Old Old Has an Anxious Dream

Matthew Miller

Dream analysts say pressure is normal,
the swirled breath in his chest, waking up wet,
sea scent twisted in his hair. He was not
drowning, but apparently parents were
arguing on saltwater's edge, whispers
about their differences, a dolphin
and a porpoise. About hidden danger—
stinging jellyfish. The beach full of holes,
but before he fell into its darkness
aunts and uncles showed up, dumping snorkels,
pool noodles and toy shovels.
Laughter dried his worried shoulders like a
beach blanket. He didn't dig anymore,
blinking awake with a fistful of sand.

Following Sunfish on the Luxapallila

John Dorroh

On late spring afternoons, the family goes fishing
at Bill Drane's camp house. I fall in love with the pier.
It rocks like a carnival ride when boats motor by.
The grown-ups tell me that noise frightens the fish.
They are scary to me sometimes. Ice clicking
in tall glasses of mixed drinks, chatter and clatter,
but it's *their* noise. So it's okay. They're grown-ups.

Lying on my belly, face three inches from brown river water,
fish tell me secrets. *Come in*, they say. *Come swim
with us.* And so I do. Who will ever miss me?

I breathe through gills on the sides of my ribs,
use caudal fin to propel me through dreams.
Brown algae like filamentous dressing for cypress
stumps, the sunfish tells me it's where he lives.

I sink back in time to a beach in San Sebastián,
Spain, where I was conceived in a salty water bath,
of purest moments of joy between two giddy adults
who eat hamburgers at the Hollywood Cafe
after making love all afternoon. I follow the fish.

There are glass bottles everywhere, many
with jagged teeth, like blood-monsters waiting
for fallen flesh. Plastic rings and bags, unsightly,
disgusting. We change courses.

We see an alligator, but she ignores us. Not hungry
enough, or interested. Turtles plop from fallen logs,
leaves form shadows, bubbles rise like champagne
from mud bottom.

I swim back to the pier. Climb onto weathered dock.
No one missed me. I should have stayed longer.

I should have
stayed longer

Aqua

Kerry Langan

The tiny tiles on the bottom and sides of the pool, so vibrantly aqua, make the girl think the water is the same color. Years later, a teacher will ask her the Spanish word for "water," and she will answer "aqua" instead of "agua." But now she is seven, a new member of the swim team, and her endurance is improving. She can swim twenty-five meters, taking only a couple breaths as her arms windmill through the water's surface, her legs kicking to propel her further, faster. The coach, standing at the end of the pool with a stopwatch, smiles as she touches the wall.

One day practice ends early and the swimmers are allowed to use the pool for recreation. The girl stands at its edge and wonders how deeply she can dive. She leans forward, bending and then straightening her knees, reaching with her overstretched arms for the water. She keeps her body straight and stiff until she's almost at the bottom of the pool. She has entered another world, a mesmerizing one where there's nothing separating her from the water or the water from her. The pool has become an enormous womb, her liquid mother slipping over her, under her, cradling her everywhere at once as she swims eight feet below the surface. Murmured sounds reach her ears, laughter and chatter, but they seem far away. If someone were to call to her, she might not recognize the sound of her own name. And she wouldn't have to answer. She is beyond everyone and everything, except the water.

She splays her arms and legs to navigate the depths, to allow her to stay under as long as possible. Blissful, she glides forward, over the aqua tiles, until her chest tightens, a tug that pulls her to the surface, where she gulps air to fill her lungs. Immediately dismayed at the noise, the shouting and the splashing, she swims to the edge of the pool and climbs out. Inhaling, she draws breath until she feels her stomach

---

swell and then dives into the tranquil, private world at the bottom of the pool. Over and over she does this, and she feels that the water is waiting to greet her, to embrace her, each time. As she's swimming to the edge of the pool, she hears the whistle signaling that it's time to leave. She silently tells the water that she'll be back in two days. Then she whispers, "Don't forget me."

In the locker room, she shivers. The air is the opposite of water, not soothing but pricking her skin. She squints at the fluorescent light buzzing overhead like a hungry mosquito and longs for the silence that lives at the bottom of the pool.

On the ride home, she tells her mother that her suit is too small and she needs a new one, an aqua one. Her mother's gaze never leaves the windshield as she inhales deeply on her cigarette and then asks, "Why aqua?"

"I want to match the water."

The mother's laugh startles the girl, and she places her hands over her ears. She does not know how to explain that she wants the water to recognize her as its own.

*there's   nothing
separating   her
from   the   water*

An Ode to the Doctor Who Saved Me

Bianca Grace

My doctor was 90 percent convinced
my legs would transfigure
into a tail

when he walked in wearing
a white jacket
and displayed an X-ray of a tumor

that inhabited my femur.
But he was 10 percent sure I might earn
a set of wings instead.

Under the surgical light,
I was a tsunami
of rapturous emotions

as I envisioned sounds
of ocean creatures
calling me home

while aware an angelic presence
stood beside the nurses.
He packed the bone

with sea coral
from the Great Barrier Reef
as the whale of a mass

ruptured my entire thigh.

When I woke from the operation
it was a salty start as I searched

for my leg under the blankets,
terrified my surgeon
grew a shark's head

while in theater
and cut my leg off
with one massive bite.

Beneath the scrubs I knew his heart
was many oceans deep.
He mapped out a perfect scar,

a gift of healing
from the trauma crashed
onto my ten-year-old body.

I walked to the ocean,
the day my crutches were recycled,
carried my tail

and fitted the blue silicone
to my waist
when I got to the water's edge.

I visited my new friends,
the turtles, the starfish, the dolphins
and my recovery room.

I am a mermaid now.
Queen of the Sea.
I swam nautical miles

back to the seaside
watching a seraph catch
the waves above me.

When I arrived back onshore
I sat with a bucket and spade
found washed up near the rocks

and buried my fears of being
made an angel too soon.

On Water

Kristine Scarrow

"Are you jumping?" my brother asks.

The others tread easily in water the color of blue spruce. My toes curl over the fiberglass edge of the boat. My kneecaps pull together like magnets, cementing me in place. The wind picks up and forms foamy whitecaps on the lake. It whips my hair into my mouth, and I work to pull my mousy blonde hair back over my shoulder. I don't know what feels worse, standing at the precipice of leaving the safety of the boat for an underworld I can't see or having the others stare at me in my Lycra bathing suit. Knobby-kneed and colt-like, with the early emergence of breasts that are both exciting and discomfiting to me, I'm uneasy with the newfound attention I'm receiving from boys in my class and strange men in the mall.

This crowd should make me feel safe: my younger brother, the children of longtime family friends who own a cabin at Turtle Lake. They are all younger than me, but their confidence makes me feel like the baby. They somersault through the water, float on their backs, and stare at the clouds making shapes in the sky. I'm a decent swimmer and spend tons of time in the water, but my feet like the feel of something solid beneath them. I do not like deep water. I see the others completely at ease. I want to be the person who can leap off vessels into unknown waters, sure of my ability to keep myself afloat, knowing the experience will change me for the better.

"Are you just going to stand there? Come on!" one of them says.

I will not be the baby. I pinch my nose, squeeze my eyes shut, and leap from the boat. The water is icy and takes my breath away. I open my eyes and see nothing. My heart gallops so quickly, it disorients me. I thrash around until I spot tiny particles floating above me from the light of the sun, turning the ominous dark to a more pleasant murky olive. I pump my legs and follow the light to the surface. I curl my legs up toward my butt, hoping my arms will be enough to keep me treading water. If I don't, I am sure my toes will become entwined with weeds; a fish will brush against my leg. There are other dangers that lurk in the black depths beneath me.

Cree legend has it that Turtle Lake is home to a sea monster. The legend says that encounters with the prehistoric creature result in mysterious disappearances. There are famed alleged sightings of this creature, mainly tales told by people fishing on the lake. Although there are theories that the creature is a possible descendant of the aquatic dinosaur, the plesiosaur, many now believe the monster is likely a humongous sturgeon that somehow made its way up from the North Saskatchewan River.

Of course, my imaginative young mind believes the Turtle Lake Monster is real. I imagine the monster slinking around us, a bottom-feeder poised to suck, its tubelike mouth choosing me—easy prey—for its afternoon snack. I wonder how others can swim so freely knowing a predator lurks in these frigid waters. My limbs grow numb despite my constant movement. I think of my mother, scarred by more than one life-threatening experience on water, and imagine her concerned about us swimming in the middle of the lake. I know from news stories and my swim instructor that growing tired in deep water can have dire consequences. I rely on a sloppy front crawl to get me back to the burgundy boat. I keep my face out of the water as much as I can.

The dad of one of the boys with us, the driver of the boat, reaches out to help pull me in. Immediately, the warmth from the sun comforts my chilled skin. My teeth chatter, making it difficult to close my blue lips. My thin, threadbare beach towel is sopped and provides a poor shield from the wind. I root myself in one of the chairs, my wet skin sticking to the PVC seat, and smile.

As a child, I am fortunate to have two aunts and two uncles, a set on either side of the family, with backyard pools. In the summer, we escape our sweltering, small house where the winter storm windows are traded for wooden screens but do little to shift the heavy, hot summer air. My father places a box fan precariously on the lip of our kitchen sink to help suck the warm air from the window into the even warmer house. My brother and I perch in front of it for relief, letting the air brush back our bangs. We talk into the spinning blades and giggle at the robotic voice that emerges.

At our relatives' houses, we swim for hours, grateful for the crystal-clear water that instantly refreshes us from the sticky sweat that coats our bodies. We practice diving, retrieve plastic rings from the bottom of the pool, listen to the tick of the pool vacuum as it meanders along the liner. Many family gatherings take place here, happy memories that show me water can be safe and playful. But even this sparkling water holds power: one day I learn that my brother almost drowned in a different backyard pool when my uncle babysat him. My uncle took his eyes off my brother and then realized it had gotten quiet. He approached the water and saw a small figure at the bottom of the pool. He fished my brother out, and they had to give him mouth-to-mouth resuscitation.

Years later, my grandpa, who could not swim, is coaxed into the pool to float in a lounge chair. He finally relaxes and enjoys the feel of the sun on his face. We stare at his protruded naked belly—a rarity for his grandchildren to see—and in another instant, an uncle tips him over, and his body becomes a boulder heading straight for the bottom of the pool. The

---

lounge chair bobs empty. I freeze in place in the shallow end and watch, helpless. It takes all my uncles and my father to pull my grandpa back up to the pool's edge. The what-ifs are terrifying. The memory still evokes tears for my mother. A joke gone bad.

It is years before I can drive, be stopped in a car, or walk on a bridge without imagining it suffering a colossal collapse. I have both daydreams and nightmares of a massive engineering fail of aeroelasticity plunging me into the water below. My vehicle slides off the bridge in perfect form, reminiscent of disaster movies. I imagine that my seat belt jams, that dirty water pours through the windows, and the vehicle is sucked down into a dark vortex. The force of the current is too much for me. I can't kick the windows and windshield out. I flail, wild, but I am trapped. It is a miserable existence to imagine these things as often as I do.

Anxiety follows me like a black cloud. In my late teens, it creates panic attacks between classes when I walk through the busy hallway termed "the tunnel" in the Arts and Science building at the University of Saskatchewan. I am the first person in my family to ever attend university, and at one point, I attend a social anxiety support group to be able to function enough to stay. Anxiety makes me vomit before job interviews, believe the worst when someone is late, robs me of opportunities I don't pursue.

Then, on the evening news, in winter 2013, the unthinkable happens. A young woman in her twenties driving on an icy Saskatoon bridge hits a snowbank that sends her car over the guardrail, hurling toward the river. Fortunately, her car does not break through the frozen river all at once. She manages to kick through her windshield and scramble to the roof

---

before swimming and pulling herself onto ice nearby before her car sinks completely. She manages to get to the riverbank with only minor injuries. This story teaches me that my fear is real. It is no longer the preposterous overblown scenario I've convinced myself it is. Bad things happen. Your worst fears can come true.

In 2015, I realize my worst fears are misplaced. I feel bruised and battered by grief after the unexpected loss of my dad to a sudden heart attack a year earlier and a hellish experience managing his affairs. The year following his death is extraordinarily painful, not only because of his absence, but because the impact of his death is the final crack in what's left of the fragile relationship with my brother. We are irreparable.

My husband and I decide to do something out of the ordinary. We book a trip to Maui for two weeks, hopeful that the lap of the ocean will soothe our aching hearts. It gets dark early in Maui. I spend most nights floating on my back in the oceanfront pool of the condo complex. I gaze at the stars, in disbelief that I stare up at the same sky so far away in Saskatchewan. I think of my dad and wonder if he knows we are here—in Maui of all places, a place my childhood self would never have dreamed of. As I float, the ocean breeze kisses my exposed cheeks and toes. This is the first time in months I feel a break from tension and sorrow. I never want to leave.

Later in the week, still in Maui, one by one, my children slip from my view, three ducklings in a turquoise sea following their father. I watch for the steady sail of the black tubes of their snorkel masks before I don my own mask. My frost-pink polished toes grip the edge of a smooth shoreline stone, the color of putty. I peer down at the coral under the salty blue North Pacific beyond my feet.

My mother is standing on a grassy incline a few yards from the water, camera in hand. She does not swim. She has her own fears of water and will not partake in this activity. The sun beats down on our pale bodies. On this February day, there is a seventy-degree difference in temperature between Kanahena Cove and Saskatoon, but the warmth does little to soothe the shiver in my knees.

I slide my feet into the unwieldy fins and crouch low. The video at the Maui Ocean Center warns of the dangers of stepping on the coral reef. Besides the risk of injury due to stings, cuts, and coral poisoning, disruption to the coral can be devastating to the reef. Conservation groups have posted signs throughout the area to educate the public and minimize risk. I attempt to slide into the temperate water without touching any of the coral, but I lose my balance and must use the seafloor to right myself. Already, I've made a misstep—one that could have consequences for decades. I berate myself, decide I should never have been so foolish, a prairie girl trying on ocean life knowing the ocean can swallow me whole if it chooses.

The rubber mouthpiece is bulky in my dry mouth. I practice breathing. A premature baby turned lifelong asthmatic, my natural breath is shallow and staccato. Snorkel breathing demands more—a long, controlled breath from only the mouth. I decide to put my face underwater. The rainbow of colors hidden under the surface does nothing to soothe me. My body tenses, my eyes flash, and I scramble to spit out the mouthpiece and gulp the sky.

My mother lowers her camera to study me. I see her concerned eyes. She isn't sure I will overcome this.

"I can't do it," I say. "I can't calm down—it feels like I'm not getting enough air. I don't know how to breathe this way."

I tread water and close my eyes. The sun absorbs the drops of water on my salt-licked face and bids me to lounge on dry land, but I want to have this experience.

Already in Maui, I've forced myself out of my comfort zone several times: ziplining in Haleakalā, a drive on the harrowing Road to Hana, whale watching on a tourist boat, and a submarine tour of the ocean floor. A carpe-diem attitude likely brought on by my dad's death. I want to add snorkeling to that list.

I take short dips with my face underneath the water, reminiscent of beginner swimming lessons, to practice this strange breathing. Nothing about this kind of breathing is automatic.

"I can do this," I decide. I splay like a starfish and let the water cradle me. I take a long pull of air through the mouthpiece until my stomach expands and exhale slowly. I do this over and over until my heart rate settles and I find that I'm finally steady. It's a mind game in which I battle for the upper hand.

I plunge back under the water and thrust myself in the direction of my family. The world under the ocean is as foreign as I've seen. I catch glimpses of yellow tang and saddle wrasse—fish I can name courtesy of our tour of the ocean center. I am in another country with my family, enjoying a part of the world I'd never imagined I'd experience.

Further north, the water darkens. I imagine that my family has drifted beyond the relative safety of the reef, sucked into that dark abyss. Perhaps their curiosity has drawn them too far from shore or maybe a current has swept them into the depths of the ocean's mouth. I imagine sharks smelling the softened scabs on my son's eczema-ridden shins or the scrape on my daughter's leg. In mere seconds, I have imagined their deaths, planned their funerals. I berate myself for allowing

---

this moment of blissful ignorance, for believing I have a right to this much joy. I wonder if I should turn back to shore.

The neon swim shorts of one of my sons propels me into action again. When they spot me, my children wave wildly at me, as mesmerized as I am by this dazzling, strange underworld. My family slices through the water toward me and pats me on the back. My husband reaches for me. We gather in a circle and clutch hands, our bellies pointed toward the dazzling bright carpet of coral polyps. There is magic underneath these waters: spiky, spongelike kingdoms in salmon, cobalt, and aubergine. Schools of open-mouthed fish move in orchestrated chaos around us. I gaze at the wonder on my children's faces and feel tears. This fairy-tale moment, this entire trip, is beyond the realm of what I dreamed possible for my life.

My feet step gingerly down the steps into the mineral pool. My legs feel unsteady. I wade slowly into the clear, warm water. My family watches me intently. They have good reason to be concerned. I have just emerged from a long spell of emergency room trips, chest pain, shortness of breath, bizarre heart rhythm problems, tachycardia, and a fatigue so intense I can barely walk. My arms are dotted with bruises from the numerous IV pokes and the repeated bloodwork to check for elevated troponin in case I have had a heart attack.

The doctors don't know what is happening; there is no firm diagnosis. As a healthy woman in my late thirties, this sudden, mysterious onset results in several urgent referrals to electrophysiology. Doctors ask for my travel history, whether I've had any recent viruses, and if I am a drug user, but I can't trace this back to anything in particular except for a recent cardiac stress test ordered by my family doctor after concerns of a high heart rate. At one ER visit, I am put in the same trauma room where my dad died. A cardiac team stands by with their equipment and paddles, their eyes glued to the monitors.

Illness changes everything. Family members take over roles that were mine, hopeful that I'll get on my feet again. When I can finally walk as far as the edge of my concrete driveway, about the distance of thirty feet, we celebrate. The Temple Gardens Hotel and Spa in Moose Jaw, Saskatchewan, boasts a geothermal mineral pool. The concentration of minerals is like other famous pools such as those found in Bath, England. The water claims to have healing properties. We come to see if the water can help me gain strength somehow—desperate people traveling for answers, hoping for a miracle cure or at least a reprieve.

This illness changes other things too—my philosophies on life, timelines for my dreams and goals. Will I die young like my dad? How many years do I have left? Will I ever be able to do the things I used to do? I am no longer worried about a crowd staring at me in a swimsuit. I'm just happy to be in the water. I no longer care about stretch marks and cellulite—just how long I get to swim for. Anxiety has become the bad memory I barely remember and am happy I shed. Instead, I want to try everything.

We wade in together. My heart races and makes me dizzy; at first, I'm unsure if this is wise or if it's too much too soon. But I give in to the water and let it hold me. Buoyant, I'm weightless. I kick and spin. I'm capable again. I'm no longer ill in this space and time, no longer bound by these newly acquired limitations. I'm my old self, but not. I am confident, sure that I will play in the water every chance I get.

The Pool

Jo Angela Edwins

Hawaii, a state
where she knew no one but her travel companions,
off snapping more pictures of statues.

Tired of walking on damaged knees,
she slid more smoothly than expected
into the years-old swimsuit, its small polka dots
tiny planets of cheer. She had not been
in a pool for years. No one here would know her,
so she would have no reason to care what they thought,
what photos they might snap of a woman large
as the horizon going carefully, two feet to each step,
down the false stone staircase into the whirlpool.

She didn't swim. Her knees weren't up to it,
so she did what she knew best, treading water
second nature by then. She used her strong arms
to push herself from side to side, avoiding
getting too close to people. The shade
of the towering hibiscus, tall as palm trees back home,
cast dark clouds on the water. Here she wasn't
afraid of any darkness, much less the sort
that cools burning skin. She closed her eyes,
let her legs lift to the surface.

Once back on the patio, she stretched out on a lounge
and snapped her own photo. *Something to admire,*
she thought, *when at last the knees give out.*

Later she would show it to her friends who would say
how beautiful she looked, how they wished they had her strength,
and she would choose to believe they meant nothing less
than what they said. Only her sister, who knew the old shame
of not fitting the world's tightly angled mold,
would say to her more than once, *I can't believe
you wore a swimsuit in public. How people must have laughed.*
But they didn't, too busy diving or backstroking,
flirting or drinking, doing what all of us
do when we don't give a damn. And she didn't
give a damn herself if anyone she did
or didn't see laughed. How sad for the sort
who would laugh at a fat, limping woman at a pool!
So many hilarious moments in the world, what poor
taste in humor.

                    She would remember most the glorious
feeling of her wet skin drying in a breeze
warm and smelling of fruit and chlorine, a scent neither
unpleasant nor perfect, just true, and she knew at that moment
the joy of the present, the power of the real.

she knew at that moment
the joy of the present,
the power of the real

Surfacing

Jo Angela Edwins

In summer, after dusk,
she stood on her dim balcony
doing something mundane—
separating heavy ferns,
shaking out dusty rugs—
when the splash startled the dark.

The complex pool,
half-hidden by a sycamore,
lay rimmed in yellow light.
Her eyes followed the thin bullet
of his body from the wet half-moon
of concrete into the canopy of leaves

that clothed the rest of his lap. His face
she imagined first smooth as a boy's,
then rugged as her old lover's, then
wet-whiskered as a walrus's.
At that she laughed so loudly
her voice shook like a stretched muscle.

When she opened her eyes, she watched
his tap-and-turn at the only end
she could see. He broke for air
under cover of the sycamore's
stiff, green-shocked limbs.
He became her deepest child,

unborn, unconceived,
thin-limbed, mute, thick-blooded,

swimming the depths of her body, as if
to steal her vital liquids,
a penalty for the quiet sin
of breathing the air it would not.

She blinked. And he was again
only a nameless neighbor
losing himself in the push and swell
of swimming a circle of water.
In time he would lift himself up and leave.
She would whisper a name through the darkness.

the splash
startled
the dark

Summer Shivers

Ed Ruzicka

My oldest was twelve the summer
I saw the ad for an above-ground pool
14' in diameter, sand filter, 42" high.
I'd get home from appointments
that stretched toward dusk with enough
light left to go into the backyard.
Bend and shovel as our stately mastiff posed
in long and doubled shade. Windless evenings
where you sweat standing, I topped grass
under a tall chinaberry, leveled surface dirt.
Then puzzled out and fit a jumble
of metal tubes on which blue plastic hung.

Although the girls would come out
to get tossed around, split sides laughing
for the splash, I think they were a little
embarrassed the way the bourgeois always are
of proletariat relatives. They preferred videos,
quiet games, talk. Maybe three friends
got in twice the whole summer. It was me
pulling weekends and doubles who'd slip in
after dark, after the children went to bed,
while my wife pretended to be absorbed
in yet another docudrama. Those nights
barn owls' drawn calls were the only other
entrance into cool on the landscape.

Weeks on end when pavement scalded bare feet,
I'd sink down with a beer in hand. Wait till
city-sky blanked enough to let stars show. Sip.

Almost ritual, that immersion, that divesting
oneself of the day. The rising shrill
of crickets, whoosh from nearby traffic
were nothing beside the waiting for
and arrival of emptiness. Sock back beer. Crawl out
to the hammock. Swing enough so wind could
rake across my chest. Shiver. Shiver under
star spikes. Under dark branches, shiver.

almost ritual,
that immersion

No Lifeguard on Duty

Benjamin Malay

Content warning: mention of suicide

I closed the screen door quietly,
barefoot across cool grass
toward the alley,
the night air thick with blossoms
and new leaves.

John and Carrie brought Jaimie,
whose skin I'd memorized
from the fifth-grade desk
behind hers,
flame-shaped scars
on one arm and neck.

We scaled chain link
to reach the dark water,
rusty metal rungs
to the diving board.

John jumped first,
shoes and all.
Converse sneakers squished
on warm concrete.
He and I had suicide in common,
each an absent father.

Carrie's ripples lured us
into the deep end,
chipped pink nail polish
glowing beneath the surface.

A police car crept toward us.
Jaimie grabbed my hand, pulled me down.
Submerged, we dodged headlights.

A makeshift family of last-born children,
alone together,
floating in a chlorinated haze.

John splashed Carrie,
screams turned to laughter,
soft echoes across blue-green water.

Back over the fence,
our clothes dripped a solitary path
in the glimmering summer night.

floating in a
chlorinated haze

Cold Spot

Karen Sadler

What surprised Cassie most about being dead was the call of the water. For her kind, it wasn't enough to die once. They wanted to drown, and drown, and then drown again. It turns out the attics and basements were empty all along, full of nothing but crumpled white sheets and moonlight glinting through filthy panes. The graveyards were stuffed with bones and teeth, yes, but nothing else. There was no pull to return to the hard things. Not when you could melt into the mud of the creek bed or slip unseen under the canoe, hot flash of silver caught for a glittering moment by July's heavy sun.

In the year since she'd died, Cassie had tried it all—disappearing into the pounding roar of Niagara Falls, obliterating herself in the waves crashing the Bondi Beach sandbanks, the sweet disassembling as she tumbled in liquid ropes over fjords, losing, if only for a second, that little sense of self that still snatched at her core. But the place she liked best, the place she went most, was the community pool she'd learned to swim in as a girl.

It hadn't changed in the twenty-odd years since she'd last sliced through the water, chlorine stinging her eyes as she darted around gangly legs and chipping flutter boards. Each day began with either Travis or Sarita, who both looked far too young to rescue anyone, unlocking the gate in the chain-link fence and shuffling over to the little building that served as an office, change rooms, and canteen. Lights on and pumps humming, they'd emerge in their standard-issue T-shirt and swim trunks just as the other lifeguards arrived, slightly hungover or high, and climbed the ladders to their little perches. Early mornings belonged to old men in Speedos pulling themselves gently along the lanes while their wives and other men's widows chatted in the shallow end between loud gulps of air as they mirrored Susan, the aquafit instructor. Susan's voice, a stilted soprano, pealed outward to the houses and apartment buildings surrounding the pool, shaking the windows and rousing the children inside eating soggy Cheerios from plastic bowls. They'd converge then, over the next hour, in that perfect turquoise rectangle, dripping sunscreen and dragging their still-damp towels behind them, claiming patches of warming pavement and run-walking to the slide, a bolted, rickety thing. The chaos that only children create ruled the remainder of each day until the sun angled further west and the smell of hot dogs grilling on balconies and yards called them home, sleepy and satisfied. Last came the adults newly home from work, still sweating from the steaming subway tunnels rumbling under the city. A quick dip in the now shadowed pool, toes pushing gently off the tile and a few lazy sips of white wine limp with ice cubes from a stainless steel bottle before padding off to the shawarma spot down the street. Then, the lifeguards' descent back to earth, quiet laughter and whispered flirting as Travis or Sarita locked the gate. Finally, as the heat settled and the bats swooped and feasted, Cassie would lie floating in the water, as much as something without a body *can* float, and consider the sky.

Nights were beautiful and lonely and occasionally frightening. Cassie never knew what might kindle the dark spark at her center, set it blazing—a streetlamp burning out, a star winking millions of light-years away, a coyote yipping in the ravine—but once ignited, it consumed. How do you flee yourself when there is nothing left to flee? She began to think of nights like these as *thrashings*. The water would churn and slap, frothing over the pool's edges as she'd struggle to drown, to sever, once and for all, the truth of her death and of her life. At the height of each thrashing, Cassie would bubble over, and in a gush of hiss and steam, blink out. Where she went during these blips of oblivion, she never knew. Hours or days later, she'd find herself back in the pool, nestled in the muffled hush of the deep end.

In this way, Cassie existed: as a ripple in the corner of Sarita's eye, as the cold spot Vlad paddled through, shivering, and as the tickle on Samir's ankle as he dove for his sister's sunglasses. And in this way, the summer passed the way summers always do: lazily, at first, like thick clouds in a windless sky, days full of melting popsicles and sweat drying under the whirl of the ceiling fan. Then, with hardly a shift, time moved quickly. Almost angrily. By Labor Day weekend, skin had burned and blistered and popped and the wasps were bitter about the coming cold. They could sense the change, despite the searing concrete under their dancing feet.

It was the last day of the swimming season, and Cassie was absorbing the vibrant, frenetic energy of the kids, almost feral now, as they splashed and screamed and jostled for a bit of space. She skimmed along the bottom of the pool, catching a glimpse of a wisp of her shadow, and gazed up at the swarm of kicking legs and floaties. She zeroed in on an open spot in the throng and arrowed up, breaking the surface and finding herself face to face with a baby.

The baby *saw her*. It regarded her with wide, unblinking eyes for a few moments, unsure what to make of the shifting, pulsing, sodden thing in front of it. It reached out a chubby hand and brushed the vibrating space where Cassie began, its mother completely oblivious to the whole exchange. And then, it *giggled*. Just a short, high-pitched belly laugh and a teasing tilt of its head, before it turned its attention back to chewing the straps on its little life jacket.

Cassie buzzed, the spark inside her blazing, but in a whole new way. To be seen! To be acknowledged! It was a gift, and Cassie was flooded with wonderings. Had she been a mother? Did she have a baby out there, somewhere? Was this baby's mother, with the soft black curls and the nose ring, a childhood friend of Cassie's? She had no idea. She couldn't remember her people, had stopped trying months ago. All she had was the pool, the only tether knotting her to before, and the thrashings.

Cassie let herself sink back to the bottom of the pool and didn't fight this time. She bubbled and hissed, steam slipping out of her core, and with a wet pop, let it all in—the gushing flood of her life and death, the whole mess and joy of it.

Laying with her mother in a hammock, half-asleep, as somewhere, an air conditioner hummed / bashing in the head of a piñata, the shock of sour candies on her tongue / Abuela making chilaquiles the mornings after family parties / Grandpa cleaning a scraped knee, so delicate with the soapy cloth / field trips to the science center, her hand on the metal ball, hair floating / calling softly into the evening for Danny, her sister's cat / staring down at her sweating palms during the calculus exam, answers blurred and useless / swigs from a flask at prom, her purple dress glinting under the disco ball / crossing the auditorium stage, gown rustling at her ankles / a spa day with Angie, steam muzzling their laughter / the first night at Matteo's apartment, half-finished glasses of rioja on the counter / Matteo, his brown fingers deep in the potted tomatoes sunning on the balcony / the news on in the background, always, red ticker tape unspooling for months on end / Matteo's lips on her forehead / the shaking / the cave of her ribs, collapsing / the nurse with the paisley scrubs and crinkly eyes / the lights and the beeping and the soft words and the hand—the warm, beautiful hand on hers as she left for the water.

Cassie came to back in the deep end, only it wasn't so deep. The water was draining, Sarita peering over the edge of the pool and fiddling with a pipe. There would be no more thrashings, Cassie knew that much. She had her people back, felt a thousand tiny pulls stretching her closer to each one. She was done dying, finally.

She spent her last morning in the pool drifting in lazy circles as the water was sucked up around her, took refuge in a shallow puddle and waited for the sun to do its work. It was a slow and strangely pleasant undoing, a warm-in-the-belly feeling of safety and anticipation. And in the last few seconds before she evaporated, Cassie felt herself rising, saw Sarita watch the sky, tasted autumn in the air.

Anonymous

Cindy Milwe

The little girl, first to swim
in the deep end of The Pond,
earned the Seahorse Patch
at Singing Oaks Day Camp—
stitched it herself on her
first red-striped Speedo.

The teenage dancer,
on the scale every morning:
95, 96, 97, 100 and then
too fast to 115, too fat
for *Cats* in the white unitard
at the Winter Garden.

After being cut at the callback,
I found myself at a counter
on Eighth Avenue—scarfing
down diner scrambled eggs
and home-fried potatoes, scraping
the butter knife across the burned toast,

peeling back the foiled seal
from the packet of grape jelly.
And I remember thinking
that no one—not one person—
knew who I was or why I was there.
It was like how I felt underwater:

gliding down the blue slide
into the brown pond on a cloudy day—
or the green pond on a sunny one—
but either way when I hit that surface
and sunk deep into the murk,
I knew no one could find me,

even for those few minutes
as I breaststroked, desperate,
hoping to make it all the way
across without coming up for air,
to finally reach the metal stairs
clamped to the man-made

concrete wall of the dock-slab.
I was alone in my breathing,
my swimming, alone in the pond
of my thoughts, my hair wild,
swirling behind me, my body
anonymous as a minnow.

*alone in my breathing,
my swimming*

Forte dei Marmi

Cindy Milwe

Content warning: sexual harassment

I took the long way to the Mediterranean Sea
loaded down by the pink mesh bag hanging

from my skinny wrist, the one my aunt bought me
at Fiorucci. The fuchsia rope created deep grooves

in my skin, heavy from my thick beach towel,
Coppertone lotion, homemade cassette tapes

and my giant Walkman, foam headphones
loose on my just-pierced ears. I chose this route

to buy my lunch: a huge nectarine with flaming
red skin and a square of focaccia, steaming

from the pizza oven, olive oil pooling
its grassy gold into the soft hills and valleys

of dough and salt, striped by rosemary. At fourteen,
I had never eaten focaccia, had never walked

alone to a beach, had never taken a public bus
to Florence or Pisa nor seen a flasher jump out

of a newsstand in his vile raincoat pointing
at my face what I did not even recognize,

and chasing me down the long alley.
But even then I knew how much I loved

the anonymity of solitude, that private quiet.
And while that felt truer than the wrought iron

chairs in the cafe courtyard and the shells
I collected at night to bring home to my sister,

if I could have spoken to the Italian boy
I passed every Friday morning manning

his father's storefront, if I could have
gathered the courage to utter even a speck

of my hard-won Berlitz Italian,
I would have bitten into the drippy

flesh of that fruit, grabbed his hand
as if to say, "Swim with me."

"Swim with me."

The Girls Are Back in Town

Callie S. Blackstone

We pin our beach towels to the line, corner
to corner, bright stripes and flowers crashing
in the sun. We walk down to the beach.
It's only half a mile. The rays slowly bake us
until we discover the relief of ocean
winds and the mirage of bare flesh.
Girls' legs are on display in bikinis;
their fathers' paunches hang over drenched swim trunks,
their mothers' eyes are shrouded by hats and dark glasses.
The women are a Greek chorus,
constantly warning their children
Get away from there! and
Put on more sunblock!
We forgot ours at home, but it doesn't matter—
we are young and we are glistening. We split up
to take our respective posts by the girls.
We weave stories about the couple that rides
horses on the shore every morning, about the roller
derby team that skates the beach path every night.
We eat up the giggles that serve as undercurrent
to the maternal yelling. The girls tell us
they're only here for the summer.
We offer our time as tour guides and experts—
we can lead them to small beaches only we know about,
identify local shells, teach them about parts
of their bodies they have yet to discover
with the mundane boys back home.

Every summer we feast on the flavors
of sun and salt, grains of sand
stuck in our teeth for days, girl smell lingering
on our fledgling mustaches—our own mothers
nag us to shave them, to trim them, to
do something! Once the girls' vacations end,
there will be others. This is the lesson they have
taught us—one after another. Summer after
summer. Girl after girl. Wetness
after wetness. We tell them that
when you look out onto the ocean
it goes as far as the eye can see—
that it feels like an eternity.

it feels like
an eternity

folk tales

Michelle Cadiz

---

there is a myth that our country
is a giant, laid down
in the ocean, fallen asleep.
you, laid down beside me,
and suddenly mountains: the slope
of your back, your shoulder blades,
your cheekbones. like the ocean
cups the shores of this archipelago,

my fingers lap
at your coastlines, secret coves
known only to the waves,
i tuck myself in
against the hollow of your throat
and breathe in your loam smell,
myself saltwater against your skin.

The Between-ness of All Things

Alex Grehy

Honeymoon island hopping,
Indonesia, each islet smaller
than the last until all
that was left between us
and the equator was a strip of
ocean, so close to the center
where time and season lay
limp and breathless
in the humid air.

On the beach, the wavelets
stroked the sand, shyly,
despite long familiarity,
taking nothing for granted.
Our fingertips brushed.

The shallow sea was warm,
but cool compared to the
heavy air, as the sky
purpled with stormlight.
We swam into deeper water,
thunder rolled far overhead,
a storm of the heavens, barely
ruffling the sea's calm surface.

We turned and floated face up
to watch the lightning flash between
clouds, worlds away from this
tranquility, supported by the
sea's saltwaters.

The rain began, dollops not droplets,
we closed our eyes, opened our mouths,
the heat of our bodies welcoming the kiss
of cold water from the cloud's icy summit.

Our hands grasped tighter, instinctive,
unwilling to be parted by the storm,
though it seemed so far away.

We drifted in the placid
betweenness of all things—
north and south,
sun and storm,
sea and sky.

The height of the sky
the depth of the ocean
and us, who were once lovers
who made our vows
before witnesses,
wife and husband
for whatever forever
lay ahead.

*the heat of our bodies
welcoming the kiss of
cold water*

Tankas without Walls

Patricia Behrens

Human body weight
is 60 percent water,
on average; heart, lungs,
muscles, and kidneys are more;
even bones are watery.

As I swim the bay
I think—*just skin separates
water from water—*
all that salt body water
from all this salt sea water.

As I swim the bay
suspended over its depths,
I feel a blood pull
to let the separation
fall away, to merge with waves,

to let the water
pull me beyond barriers,
so rocked by motion
I swim to a place, a time
where everything is water.

Swimming out the Squall

Patricia Behrens

Like wind ghosts, squall gusts
ruffle up the water's surface
and toss me
like machine wash
in underwater roiling.
I lurch and spin and almost
flip, turning to breathe,
as if drunk on the salt margarita
of the waves.

Rain pelts my cap,
my shoulders, my face,
slides into my mouth
with every breath.
My goggles fog and I
surrender to motion,

feel myself drawn back
to the summer I was ten,
the ozone zing, the drizzle
the long, steady rain
that pinged holes in the water
as I dove from rocks,

entering with the rain,
when I learned all squalls pass,
when everything was play,
and rainy days
were what I wanted.

Swimming Lessons

Charlene Stegman Moskal

When Florence tried to teach me to swim
she would lie to me.
She stood in the green Atlantic water
as the waves softly crashed about her shoulders.
It was never too deep for her
but fathoms for me.

I would lie prone on my back
across her outstretched arms.
I was terrified.
Don't drop me
Don't let me go
and she said she wouldn't
and then she did.

And I would sink as I struggled against the saltwater
that attempted, against my flailing, to hold me up,
and she would laugh at me.

I kept going back for more.
I did not want the ocean to win;
I wanted to do as my cousins did,
jump in and out of the waves with abandon
one arm and then the other stretching out
to claim their dominion over the vast expanse.
I wanted to be like them,
kick my feet, propel myself forward,
be as comfortable in as I was out of the water.

So I kept going back for more—

I wanted to believe this time I could trust her.
And every time she lied
and every time she laughed.

We both gave up, she tired of the game
and I determined I could do it myself.
Eventually I did,
not well, but I haven't drowned yet.
There are no waves in my pool
and I know I can always touch the bottom.

be as comfortable
in as I was out of
the water

Underwater

Charlene Stegman Moskal

I have never understood those
who choose to swim underwater—
it is unnatural to voluntarily
put yourself somewhere
you cannot breathe or see clearly or hear.

When I swim I keep my head above water,
rarely challenge myself to attempt
what appears enjoyable to others;
when I try, I take maybe four or five strokes
before I panic.

I prefer to float and as I write this I realize
I have written a metaphor for my life;
I float, keep my head above water,
make sure the passageways are available,
nothing closed off, alien to life.

I refuse to put myself in dangerous waters
I keep close to shore—
only swim in quiet coves or lakes or pools,
places without the treachery of waves,
or the flotsam and jetsam of others' lives.

I wish those braver than me well;
I am content to cheer them on,
watch with all my senses intact
as they play at being fish in an element
we gave up billions of years ago.

I guess the primordial me just couldn't wait
to lift my head and get out of the water.

It's on Them

Charlene Stegman Moskal

In the drawer right below my "necessaries"
are two bathing suits.
They know better than to wait for me.

I think it's been about five years, give or take,
since either of them found their way into water;
one is red and the other a floral pattern of blue and black.

I see no need for them.
I have a swimming pool surrounded by a cinder block wall
high enough to keep prying eyes out

and I really don't care.
At my age if anyone is curious enough to look
it's on them—

all the nightmares about what their body
will become when they are really old.
So to the inquisitive, I say good luck.

It is my summer pleasure to sit on the side of the pool
and slowly lower myself into the make-believe aqua water
to float, look at the sky, make pictures in the clouds

and feel ageless
light and beautiful
with my memories of you and you and you

I let my hair flow around me;
a halo of gray that becomes Botticelli's Venus.
I am no longer a Philip Pearlstein naked old woman.

In the water I am a vessel with long limbs
and a peach tan body,
desirable and as young as I choose to be.

and feel ageless
light and beautiful
with my memories of
you and you and you

wishing
we were
anywhere
but the
high school
swimming
pool

Alejandra Medina

---

8 a.m., freshman year, fifteen silhouettes awkward beside the pool. The water ripples as it churns through a filter, giggling at us. Our reflections are distorted watercolor interpretations of angular limbs shielding exposed flesh: chubby thighs, knobby knees, shoulders acne-red. We've got curves that overflow, our bodies unbound by the polyester swimsuits we tug and pull. We don't love us quite yet.

That comes after we dive in and learn to cut through water like a blade—sharp, strong. When we learn to push through, demand space. Feel our hearts pump us full of adrenaline, our lungs burning to gasp and claim those summer gusts rolling over our heads. We learn to feel alive, every cell burning, not because the sun is slowly awakening and breaking into frag-mented fingers that caress us, hot through the chlorine blue, but because we've learned to dance through water;

bodies rhythmic
below the surface, sturdy
and unsinkable.

Blood in the Pool

Mariah Eppes

The story goes that when my twin sister and I were four years old, my dad strapped floaties around our torsos and threw us into the pool. We had a full-size, in-ground pool—an incredible luxury in an otherwise modest house—and he wanted us swimming as soon as possible. In Las Vegas, where we lived, you could take advantage of such a luxury from April through October.

By eight years old, I was a strong, confident swimmer. The point of swimming for me was not to go fast, but to play games. See how long you could stand on the raft without falling. Jump on the raft and get the biggest splash. Count how many spins you could do before landing in the water. My sister and I, taking turns, keeping score. I did handstands underwater, figured out how to hold my breath so I was less buoyant and could sit cross-legged on the gritty pool floor, stared up at the surface through my goggles, pretending I was a sea creature.

Falling didn't hurt when you fell in water. I was fearless pushing off the wall, rocketing forward to see how far I could go before I had to start kicking. I was powerful as I watched how my movements underwater affected the surface—ripples and bubbles and miniature waves. The textured concrete around our pool was so familiar I was not afraid of slipping on it. I liked to do front flips from the edge into the deep end, then see if I could hold my breath long enough to touch the bottom. I dragged my fingertips across the floor, to prove that I'd done it, then pushed off with my feet toward the air just as the strain in my lungs began to set in.

And then there was the special treat of summer: the night swim. Our pool light, a round, warm bulb at one end of the rectangle, lit the water an icy blue-green color. Some illusion of this light turned the night sky an unearthly purple. For some time, my sister and I didn't know what was causing it, only that night swims came with a purple sky.

In another game of ours, this same pool light was a portal. We placed our hands, one at a time, over the bulb. Kicking and splashing up a storm, we raced back toward the opposite end of the pool, and when we reached the other side, we were in WaterWorld, an undersea kingdom where there were endless plots for us to enact. Hours could go by this way. When we were finally bored or tired or sunburned, we sat around a small iron table in the backyard until the breeze made us cold under damp towels.

But swimming changed. It was changed, like everything, by my period. My sister and I were aligned in unspoken understanding. There was at least one week per month when the pool didn't seem very comfortable. When we refused to swim, my father said, "But it stops when you get in the water." I was not convinced. My body was not only me anymore. It did things without my permission. I did not know what it was capable of.

"It's just us," my father insisted. "You're at home!" He didn't understand that I was not afraid of *other people* seeing blood in the pool, *I* was afraid of seeing blood in the pool. The kicking and splaying of legs was not a move I made unthinkingly ever again.

More changes followed, relentlessly. The next was bathing suits. Bathing suits now had to be "cute," and certainly two pieces. Critically, the bathing suit needed enough padding to render nipples completely invisible. My sister knew, without words, to give me a once-over and a thumbs-up: silent confirmation that there was no evidence of a body, just the acceptable suggestion of one. From age eleven on, I couldn't wear bathing suit bottoms without shorts. My upper thighs were inexcusable. I didn't want to see them.

These bathing suits were not made for kicking, hard, off of pool walls and rocketing through water. The force of water gets easily under a two piece, lifting it away from your chest.

"You're at home!" But I was not afraid of *other people* seeing my top come off in the pool, *I* was afraid of seeing my top come off in the pool. Shame was waiting in the threat of exposure—it would be shameful even if I was the only one to see it.

There was now work to do before swimming. Shaving in the shower, close inspections of skin, mirror examinations of how far my stomach extended over the top of my bottom piece. The water itself was almost a hassle. There was too much that needed to be controlled in an environment that resisted controlling. My body was restricted into a much-reduced range of motion. When I was a teenager, our pool was primarily a place to attempt tanning (futilely) after a brief swim. I often just sat at the edge, jean legs rolled up, and swished my feet back and forth, unwilling to go through all the effort to be pool-approved.

My dad had the pool redone when I was sixteen.

When I went out to swim in the inaugural season after the renovation, my feet didn't recognize the new concrete texture—would it grip me? It seemed more slippery. I lowered myself down the three steps into the shallow end. The floor was less gritty. The walls were smoother. These were not the tiles I had memorized, drawing over them with my index finger, closely watching single drops separate from my hands and rush down to rejoin the water at the surface. While the work was being done, the pool accessories had been piled up out of the way. They were dirty and cobwebbed. I didn't want to touch them. The old raft was folded in a corner of the back-yard, dry and cracked by the sun.

My body still had a memory of the energy expelled here. It felt like my body wanted me to *do* something, to wear my-self out. My body remembered that we could have fun here; kicking and splaying of legs. Didn't we use that raft for some-thing? Did that pool light lead somewhere once? Another world? Did I leave something there, something I should have kept?

But I couldn't think of anything to do in the new pool be-sides swim laps. *How unimaginative*, I thought, wading in. Then I kicked off the wall slowly, so as not to disturb the bikini top.

Did I leave something there, something I should have kept?

Confessions of a Non-Swimmer

Barbara Simmons

My answer to jumping
into the deep
or any end of any pool
has simply been
not to.
I've never learned to swim,
begetting, I suppose,
my hesitancy to dive into
conversations or relationships:
The former found me paddling toward my words
like weighted objects I'd been told to find,
but only if I'd dive. So, I'd emerge before the words
could choke me. The latter found me fearful of
submersion into someone else's waters,
a baptism into who they thought
I should have been.
I'm swimming in my thoughts to
days when, from the bleachers,
I would listen to the scratchy sounds of orders
from the local sergeant tasked with teaching
high school girls to swim.
I clutched my note from home, the one
my mother wrote each Tuesday
marked with "monthly" on it, our
personal request to let my own flow
take me out of water, onto land.
Now, I wonder what it would have felt like
if I'd learned to swim.

Would all the sunken words
have floated to the surface, would I
have uttered what I'd thought about,
knowing that I'd already seen below
where thinking dragged me
diving into life, well
before my body thought me ready?
Would I have pulled
away from several almost drownings
saving what I'd glimpsed of
me when I sat still, alone, intact,
on my own shore, or, at the very least,
feeling the bottom of the pool,
scraping my knees, opening my eyes,
sensing I had something to stand on?

all the sunken words
floated to the surface

Underside

Suyin Du Bois

Here I am,　　　bobbing　　　　fluorescent pulse
　　　in the warm　overturned belly
　　　　　of the boat.　　So　　　wide-eyed

my seahorse hippocampus,
　　　　womb-memory　　　　still lingers
　　in my limbs.　My small body　　　　knows

　　　this feeling,　　bundled　　　by the sea,
palms　　　　lapped　　　　on its hull-shaded surface.
　　The solid seam　of the life jacket

　　　　　　under my arms　hoists
　　me　from an　　　unconsidered seabed.
Luminescent shoals　at my thighs,

　　　tiny shivers　　of fish,
　welcome party　　　to my first wade
　　　into the shallows,　keep me company.

In the　drift of second guesses,　at the mercy of moon tide,
　　I memory-float　my full-grown　body here,
　　　to　　this　　cellular safety,

　　　　to remind　my lungs　of their buoyancy.
　I forget　the boat　capsizing,
　　my parents,　swum-out and sodden,

paradox awash,　seeing not inverted vessel　but casket,
　　　calling *au secours* to save the baby beneath.
　I recall　entrusting　every cell to the　moment.

I don't remember　　being saved.
I don't remember　needing　to be saved.

The Light and the Lake

Dana Getka

He's in all this water here. He's in the breeze, in the tide crumbling on the rocks. Hollow mouth of the wave. Softening stones, year after year after year.

He's here, alright. He never left, so it seems.

577.86 (−0.27)

The month he was born, the water level was 577.86, a decrease of 0.11 percent over the previous year. He came into a downward sloping world, that is true. Fell flat into it. Whether he floundered or started to tread, we'll never know. What we do know is that these things don't last long. Soon enough the waters were rising. 578.47. 578.92.

He let them carry him along. 1897. 1898. 1899.

When the new century came, he was sleeping. The groan of the waves crowding his little ears, shaped like a perfect pair of seashells.

His mother watched him as he slept.

Something troubled in the knit of his pale, porcelain brow.

578.05 (+0.19)

We start at the beginning, but it was written from the very end.

579.06 (+0.01)

A year ticks by. We watch it happen. One little brother, and then another soon followed.

The first left to lie in the sandy Indiana soil, the second a stalwart barnacle clinging to his brother's shadow. They went everywhere together, these two. Matching skinned knees. Fingers hooked in Mama's skirt. Their breathless hearts beat in tandem, four little lungs brimming with saltwater tears, or quiet laughter.

Yet the youngest soon learned that he was different from his brother. He was the baby of the family and knew it, liked to cause trouble, to be a loud shout in the morning. He smiled often and saw it mirrored in his mother's face.

His older brother seemed a world apart. Lost in the copse of trees in his mind, like the one on the edge of the farm. Eyes taken from Scandinavian glass, they rarely left the ground. When they did, he squinted at the sun. Long and hard. Trying to discern its essential question, the one he knew it to have swallowed whole.

Still, they were rarely apart. If only because there was nothing else to do.

579.04 (−0.02)

The tender geometries that brothers trace through the world. The youngest hoped they might stay together forever. The eldest wondered if this might be his fault.

579.28 (−0.10)

There was something magnificent about his father, he thought, watching him return from the fields at dusk. The last light of day crowned his fair, rugged head with the palest violet; darkness pooled across the planes of his face. Thick muscle gave him the look of a bear, yet he maneuvered the twilit world with a care that seemed incongruent, an inborn gentleness left over from some former life.

His son admired this quality, looked for it during his father's frequent temper-spikes. It was there in the tight skin pulled across his knuckles, in the rattle of the crockery, in the shout and slam of the door. His father's anger never reached the bone-level. It wasn't true to his nature, and the eldest knew this, assured his sniffling brother that it was only a spell a witch had cast, that their real father would return soon.

And he always did. Worn from his labors in the field, but ready with a smile, a quip, a ruffle of the hair. He scooped up his eldest there in the dusk, his quiet shade of a son, blending into the darkness. His father admired the strength in his little body. The impossible echoes of his own mouth and eyes in the face of another.

The boy looked at him silently, lovingly.

579.30 (+0.26)

Sitting alone in the long-haired grass, miles from the shore, he thought he could hear the waves. They rumbled at the edge of his consciousness, spoke to him in a language he could but barely understand. It sounded like the voice of his father, of his father and his two workmen. The resonant tones of the old country, something between a song and a scolding.

He wrapped the grass around his fingers. Tried to make it look like his mother's hair, coiled in a thick braid around her head. The waves sang to him. He didn't know what they were saying, but he knew it to be true.

578.36 (−0.15)

Language came slowly to him. Words passed over his head, all på svenska, the quick lilting speech of his mother, the lumbering laughter of the farmhands, but he took no part in it. Unable to speak, he sat in silence as thick as a pool of treacle. Getting him to talk was akin to extracting a molar. You had to get him to open his mouth first.

His mother was troubled by this but tried not to show it.

578.14 (–0.22)

What she did not realize was that language began in his hands. They cupped grasshoppers, cottonwood leaves, glacial erratics reduced to pebbles. So gently he held them, his palms pink and trembling. Like he might break them. Like the anxious tremor in his body, stilled only in sleep, might turn them to dust.

578.95 (–0.35)

Life cripples the happiest families. Another thick headstone, another shovelful of sandy soil. Prayers in Swedish. Trim of stone flowers. When his father died, he was too young to understand it. Too young to understand that he was now the light, and his family the lake.

He was six years old. He held his mother's skirt so tightly it left an ache in his fingers for days after.

579.76 (+0.81)

Years trickled by. 1907. 1908. 1909.

His bones grew, and with restless certainty he creaked his way closer to the sun. He wore a hat like a proper young man, trying to set a good example for his brother, but still the tops of his cheeks turned a chastened pink. The sun thought kindly of him. It ran golden fingers through his golden hair, mimicked with a laugh the squint he gave it. Wondered what he saw in it that it didn't see in itself.

579.73 (–0.03)

A perpetual stitch in his brow. This is how history would remember him.

579.19 (−0.57)

His spine felt warm with the sun's attention as he wandered the shore. He longed to shed his jacket, but he was nearly to the school, and anyway he felt once again the desire to walk through the discomfort, to suffer, although on whose behalf he wasn't sure. Sweat stuck to his starched collar. He looked yearningly toward the water, felt its cool breeze rush through the thin fabric of his shirt.

The waves lunged for him. He felt the tug at the center of his ribs.

579.30 (+0.11)

Indiana has forty-five miles of Lake Michigan shoreline. If you look at a map you'll see it: a bent elbow, or a crooked smile. If you look closer you'll see him, carving a path through the sand. Left ear lifted toward the waves.

578.29 (+0.55)

It's hard to be fifteen and have no voice. He sensed this in a vague, dire way, holding his words like a dry pebble under his tongue. His classmates flitted from one corner of the room to the other, chattering gulls, anxious to get their voices into the air, and he sat in the midst of it all, silent as a boulder.

No man is an island. He did not believe this to be true. He was Donne's clod washed away by the sea, deposited here among the seabirds, who walked across him as though he were a stepping-stone. He tried to speak. The words of the old country gurgled up instead.

His shoulders hurt. The schoolmistress told him to stop frowning, but he wasn't frowning, he was thinking about the end to suffering and whether it existed or whether it kept going and going like the water toward the horizon. He despaired at the idea of infinity. He didn't know how to say this to the schoolmistress.

He tried to unknit his brow. It didn't work.

577.93 (−0.17)

It had been many years since he left flowers at his father's grave. He was a child then and wept little hiccupping tears as he dropped the crushed bouquet of larkspur in front of the stone. His mother scolded him. (She later regretted it.) The wind blew warm through the cemetery trees.

You're the man of the family now, she said to him, *på svenska.* Your father is watching you.

A heavy weight upon such narrow shoulders. Behind a nearby gravestone, his brother giggled. For some reason relishing the way grief's burden crimped the older boy's back.

578.19 (+0.26)

Years later, as a teenager in need of comfort, he would remember her words differently: *Your father is watching over you.* It was a fiction, and he knew it, yet it never stopped him from recreating the past in a gentler hue, if only in his mind.

He ran his fingers over history, again and again, until it was smooth like a lake stone. It was always cold to the touch. He did not know why.

578.46 (+0.27)

Summer afforded him the chance to be weightless.

He lugged his newly lanky body over the dunes, dug his fingers and heels into the shifting sands. The grasses whistled their greeting. The waves murmured their approval.

He crossed the shore, shedding his shoes, his collar, his shirt. Like a skin peeling away. The water came to meet him. It tugged on his ankles—and in he went.

The rush of coolness pulled on his lungs like a thread. His skin ached for a moment, overheated, and sweat peeled into his wake as he swam, pushing his way through the initial thrill of cold. His mind entered a blank space, the pause between words. Behind his eyes he saw a clear, dark blue.

He came up for air. Surprised to see the world still whole, unchanged in his absence.

578.74 (+0.28)
He liked being in the water, liked to be alone with the lake, listening to the waves and their quiet, friendly banter. Sometimes his brother tagged along, which he deplored, but there was nothing to be done about it. His mother insisted they spend time together. One hand kneading her sore hip, she looked between the two, the eldest fidgeting, the younger blinking pale glass eyes.

Be a good older brother for once, she told him, and then hastily reversed course. Tried to wind the skein of those last two words, which were not meant to leave her lips.

It stung like a sunburn. He said nothing and trudged back out the door.

Needless to say he spent the rest of the day alone.

578.58 (−0.16)
Summer wore on, growing threadbare in places.
His skin warmed beneath the sun but never darkened. It turned pink-mottled in places, the tops of his cheeks in particular, which rose close to the sun when he smiled and lingered there as he thought upon some happy incident of the

past. They were precious to him, these memories of another world, a land where his father was alive and life seemed ready with meaning and magic.

He liked to float on his back and think upon such times. Whether the memories were real or the fictions of a lonely mind, it didn't matter. They succored him there under the afternoon sun. They buoyed him, and he floated on, imagining he might stay and float there forever.

But his brother's giddy shout, delighted at some feather or shell—wasn't he too old for such childish things?—would come like a breaker over the calm surface of his mind, and he would sink beneath the water, lead-laden, until his head filled with blue.

579.40 (+0.62)

The lake rose to meet him the year he turned seventeen. A tenth of a percent of an increase, remarkable. He grew, too, the last stretch, or so it seemed. When he stood, he just kept going.

His mother was secretly pleased with this. She liked to be dwarfed when they stood, arms almost touching, in the old wooden pews. He looked more and more like his father every day, she thought. Same hands, gentle and agitated. Same set to the jaw when trouble brewed. She glanced at him now, listlessly turning the pages of a hymnal. His knee bounced. His lower lip, fuller than the moon, pinched tight between his teeth.

579.48 (−0.19)

He brushed his hands on his trousers, palms sticky with sand. He'd buried the gull deep where the water couldn't find it, where he couldn't find it, as though putting it out of sight would erase the image of its splayed, broken wings from his mind.

He squinted at the sky, looking for the answer to its unjust demise. He could find nothing.

For hours after, his heart felt stuck between the cracks of his ribs.

578.97 (–0.43)

He doesn't know that he will die but supposes that it might happen someday.

That it might be some day soon never occurs to him. The grasses don't tell him this. He does not hear it in the restless murmuring of the waves. The sun, his golden-spired guardian, cannot bear to look him in the eyes and say it. And so he wanders the shore, unaware, fingers trailing through the dusk.

It is still summer. Life will go on, as it always has. It must . . .

579.54 (+0.57)

Yet the days are growing stingy with their wares, withholding a moment of sun, now a minute, now close to an hour. He can feel the change in his skin, the way it longs for the light, strains against his bones toward the cloud cover.

This must be the worst time of year, he thinks, when summer nears its end, but does so slowly, dragging out the torment, postponing the inevitable. All good things end in summer. His mother will know this soon.

578.85 (+0.31)

As he sits on the shore, trousers rolled and caked with sand, he thinks about the future.

He has graduated high school. College awaits him now, with its stiff collars and stiff conversation. Boys who will judge him, girls who will wonder fruitlessly at the mind behind the silence. He worries and thrills at the idea. To him this future seems the horizon line, infinitely distant, its waters dark and fathomless, empty and cool.

It is like the lake before him now, the ink of evening spilling across its surface. Its face opaque, its depths unknowable.

578.97 (+0.04)
As he stands he has a vision of himself drowning. Of the last light disappearing above him, lost between the interweaving fingers of the waves.

One final gasp for breath, then darkness.

578.98 (+0.01)
He trudges over the dunes, brow knit, mouth set. And he takes an odd comfort in this snapshot of the future, knows without knowing that this is how he will die, someday, many years hence. He feels this deep in the marrow of his bones. He feels that God must be whispering it to him now, over the hush of the waves. Beneath the distant cry of the gulls.

578.98 (+0.00)
He hopes his father will be there to meet him when it happens.

580.12 (−0.49)
R.D. #2, Chesterton, Indiana.

Deeply regret to inform you that Lieutenant J—— is officially reported as killed in action, September 12, 1918.

lost between
the interweaving
fingers   of the
waves

dreams of
luminous
gill-bearing
aquatic craniate
animals may prove
surprisingly
therapeutic when
experiencing
profound grief

Jane Ayres

---

untwisting the living canvas
it felt dirty on my skin
as if the sea was thick
textured with surface dust
the day sliding away
in a shoal of memories
harsh debris floating by
            - a lighter touch -
as waves spewed
phosphorescent fish droplets
onto the shore
where crowds gathered

watched
gasped in wonder

so many

I swam toward them
each stroke eating water
& emerged
amazed

for a time
it helped me

forget

My Dad Swims His Evening Laps

Matthew Miller

A stethoscope hangs over his shoulders,
swings across his buttoned-up oxford shirt.

All day, he enters windowless rooms,
examining those hurt by illness, or bad decisions.

No surprise then, he sheds it all on summer evenings,
six o'clock, splashing into the pool

with one shining swan dive. His head ducks,
disappearing into quiet water split seconds

before impact. Always the good doctor, he begins
working off the work, scrubbing away worries

like germs, like the antibacterial washing that follows
every visit with his patients. Inside, we wait impatiently

for dinner. He touches the wall, circling.
Shoulders turning, pulling at the sun rays floating

in front of his goggled eyes. Stopping to sputter
a breath, he flips and flutters deeper under.

Three more lengths and done. On the deck,
he loops his suit over the rail, dripping onto the rocks.

Completely free, he chooses new clothes. He breathes deep
and comes to the table clean, ready to fill his plate with us.

Our Family Swims across the Lake

Matthew Miller

We dumb ones, young cousins, choppy strokes and shrieks
shattering mirrored water, lapping the muck
on shore. We push off.
Shaking heads, hands and stiff shoulders,
our aunts and uncles shoot slowly through
the smooth surface. They all know
the silent rhythm they must rend
through unruffled waves. Speedoed, Uncle Gordon torpedoes
our splashing throng. He's lifeguard trained, but we still strain
to keep his pace. Our moms and dads let their brother go.
Competitive but grizzled,
they know their limits
and the length of this lake's trial.
Next year, they'll all strip to Speedos—
mocking him since they can't beat him, but this year
it's just stroke after stroke,
breath after breath. Their bodies slide between
ours, passing us with long gasps, spitting out
the grimy water.
The youngest of us quit,
board the boat. Grandma wraps towels around our cold shoulders.
We watch as our aunts and uncles rise through the sunset,
stepping onto the sands of the shoreline.

Good Heat

Emma Bider

This is good heat.

It is August on the dock. I lie on my back trying to calculate the exact moment when sweat is about to bead along my collarbone before I rise and dive into the water like a dark-winged loon in search of bottom-dwelling insects.

It is a cloudless day, and this is good heat. A light breeze sounds the leaves and dusts the water with its gentle touch.

A week ago, I wanted to bury myself in the cool soil underneath my maple trees. The sun was angry, the pulsing humidity unbearable. Today it has calmed, and we play this game, me waiting until it has touched every part of me before I surrender to the liquid oasis of the lake. I let the sun win every time.

The surface of the water is warm. I let my body sink until my toes dip into a layer of colder water. It fills me with a tingling joy. No clouds to betray blue sky, just this good heat reflecting on the water, dancing on my hair, my lips, my cheeks.

When there are others here, when invited, I never want them to stay too long. They are loud, cannoning into the lake and sharing its relief with those of us on the dock. Later, they are quiet, reading, or asking about a show, have you watched it, should we see a movie in town, should we leave this perfect place to drown in a different kind of submission?

I know I should want to share this world, this good heat and blue sky that makes me realize the roundness of the earth, this layered lake water with its worlds. But I don't. Maybe I'm too cautious.

I heard somewhere that divinity is only possible in community and I believe it. My community is here. I dive into the lake water and greet the tadpoles and mosses, wood ducks, and once an osprey, particles of sand and rock and feel expanded by the water kissing my neck, establishing correctly that it is with kin, separated only by hair and skin.

In one moment, it's like bed sheets drying in evening summer air, then like a breeze through a morning window, then like the thrumming of a barn swallow's wings, just on the edge of hearing.

It is good heat on a clear day with sweat braiding my forehead and I am part of it all. I move through the air above the lake, caught in the sacred, the momentary, the fleeting ache of body waiting to touch water.

*the fleeting ache
        of body waiting
                to touch water*

Contributors

Jane Ayres (she/her) is a UK-based neurodivergent writer who completed a creative writing MA at the University of Kent in 2019 at fifty-seven. Her work can be found in *Lighthouse*, *Streetcake*, *The North*, *The Forge Literary Magazine*, and elsewhere. In 2021, she was nominated for Best of the Net, was shortlisted for the Aesthetica Creative Writing Award, and won a Laurence Sterne Prize. Her first collection, *edible*, was published by Beir Bua Press in 2022. You can find her online at janeayreswriter.wordpress.com.

Patricia Behrens was born in Massachusetts and now lives on Manhattan's Upper West Side. She is a lawyer and writer and also enjoys open water swimming. Her work has recently appeared in publications such as *Naugatuck River Review*, *Split Rock Review*, and *The Literary Bohemian*.

Emma Bider (she/her) is a writer and PhD student living in Ottawa. She writes poetry and speculative fiction about the future of our world in the climate crisis. Her first book of short stories, *We Animals*, was published in 2020. Her short stories have been published in *Capsule Stories*, *PACE Magazine*, and *State of Matter*. Her poetry has been published in *3 Moon Magazine* and *Northern Otter Press*.

Callie S. Blackstone writes both poetry and prose. Her work appears or is forthcoming in *Plainsongs*, *Lily Poetry Review*, *Rust and Moth*, *Prime Number Magazine*, *West Trestle Review*, and others. Callie is a lifelong New Englander. She is lucky enough to wake up to the smell of saltwater and the call of seagulls every day. You can find her online home at calliesblackstone.com.

Michelle Cadiz is a poet, biologist, and climate activist. She was born, raised, and resides in the Philippines. You can find her on Twitter at @michellyfishal.

Eve Croskery is a writer, mother, and primary school teacher. She lives in Auckland, New Zealand, with her partner and two young children, who have helped her to rediscover her creativity and passion for writing. You can read more of her work on Instagram at @evepoetry_.

John Dorroh has never had to use a defibrillator, nor has he fallen into an active volcano. He did manage to bake bread with Austrian monks and consume a healthy portion of their beer. Two of his poems were nominated for Best of the Net. Others have appeared in journals such as *FERAL*, *Burningword Literary Journal*, *Tilde~*, and *Selcouth Station*. His first chapbook, *Swim at Your Own Risk*, was published in 2022.

Suyin Du Bois (she/her) is a poet and tech startup consultant of mixed Chinese-Malaysian and Belgian heritage who lives in London with her South African husband. There are many places she calls home. She studied for her BA in English literature and creative writing at the University of Warwick. Find her on Instagram at @suyin.du.bois.

Jo Angela Edwins has published in various venues, including *Mom Egg Review*, *Grand Little Things*, *Halfway Down the Stairs*, and *Amethyst Review*. She has received awards from Winning Writers, Poetry Super Highway, and the SC Academy of Authors and is a Pushcart Prize, Forward Prize, and Bettering American Poetry nominee. She lives in the Pee Dee region of South Carolina and serves as poet laureate for the region.

Mariah Eppes (she/her) is a writer in New York City. You can find more of her work around the internet and at bird byrocket.com. She's on Twitter at @BirdByRocket and Instagram at @bird.by.rocket.

Belle Gearhart is an emerging writer and a creative writing student at the University of Redlands. A displaced New Yorker, they live in Southern California with their child, partner, and pet rabbit Scully.

Dana Getka is a master's student pursuing a degree in history. Her work circles around notions of memory and the archive during the early twentieth century.

Bianca Grace is a poet from Australia. She is completing a graduate certificate in editing and electronic publishing. She is a reader at *Full House Literary*. Her work has appeared in *Anti-Heroin Chic*, *Selcouth Station*, *Capsule Stories*, *The Daily Drunk Mag*, *Postscript Magazine*, and elsewhere. Follow her on Twitter at @Biancagrace031.

Alex Grehy's sweet life is filled with narrowboating, rescue greyhounds, singing, and chocolate. Her work has been published in a range of anthologies and zines worldwide, including *Red Penguin Collections*, *Toasted Cheese Literary Journal*, and *Gnashing Teeth Publishing*. Her work is also available via a global network of prose and poetry dispensers run by French publisher Short Edition. She is recognized for her vivid prose, thought-provoking poetry, and original view of the world.

Chelsie Kreitzman lives in Kentucky with her husband, two young sons, and a tuxedo cat named Cookie. Her poetry has been published in literary journals, including *Poetic Sun*, *Stick Figure Poetry*, *The Purpled Nail*, and *MockingOwl Roost*.

Kerry Langan has published three acclaimed collections of short fiction, the most recent being *My Name Is Your Name* by Wising Up Press. Her short fiction has been published in dozens of literary magazines, including *StoryQuarterly*, *Cimarron Review*, *West Branch*, *American Literary Review*, *The Seattle Review*, *Other Voices*, *Reflex Fiction*, *Fictive Dream*, *Syncopation Literary Journal*, and others. Her fiction has been anthologized often, including in *Solace in So Many Words*, *XX Eccentric: Stories about the Eccentricities of Women*, and others.

Benjamin Malay works in a variety of mediums to create deeply personal images of people and places, embracing imperfect memory and fleeting life. In 2017, his creative nonfiction work "Agates" was featured in the Solitude's Spectrum issue of *Cahoodaloodaling*. Benjamin's nonfiction short story "Postcard from Reno, May 1980" was published in the January 2019 edition of *Cagibi Express*. He is the sole proprietor of a fine art framing business in Seattle, Washington. You can find him online at benjaminmalay.com.

Alejandra Medina is a Latina writer, born and raised in Los Angeles, California. She is a WriteGirl alumni and recipient of a Scholastic Art and Writing Award, and her work has appeared in *Lucky Jefferson*, WriteGirl's *Lines & Breaks*, *The Incandescent Review*, *Unpublished Magazine*, *Alebrijes Review*, and elsewhere.

Matthew Miller teaches social studies, swings tennis rackets, and writes poetry—all hoping to create home. He and his wife live beside a dilapidating orchard in Indiana, where he tries to shape dead trees into playhouses for his four boys. His poetry has been featured in *Whale Road Review*, *River Mouth Review*, *EcoTheo Review*, and *Ekstasis Magazine*.

Cindy Milwe is a writer, teacher, and swimmer who lives in Venice, California, with her husband and three children. Her work has been published in many journals and magazines, including *5AM*, *Alaska Quarterly Review*, *Poetry East*, *Poet Lore*, *The William and Mary Review*, *Flyway*, *Talking River Review*, and *The Georgetown Review*, among others. She has poems in two anthologies: *Another City: Writing from Los Angeles* (City Lights, 2001) and *Changing Harm to Harmony: Bullies and Bystanders Project* (Marin Poetry Center Press, 2015). In 2018, her poem "Hunger" was selected as first prize winner for the Myra Shapiro Poetry Prize, sponsored by The International Women's Writing Guild. She was awarded first prize for her poem "Legacy" by the Martha's Vineyard Institute of Creative Writing and received the Parent-Writer Fellowship. Her poem "Memorial" was nominated for a Pushcart Prize. Her first full-length collection, *Salvage*, was published in 2022 by Finishing Line Press.

Charlene Stegman Moskal is a teaching artist for the Alzheimer's Poetry Project in Las Vegas, Nevada. Charlene is published in numerous anthologies, print magazines, and online publications, including *TAB Journal*, *Humana Obscura*, *Kosmos Journal*, *Griffel*, *Gyroscope Review*, and *Sandstone & Silver: An Anthology of Nevada* Poets (Zeitgeist Press, 2020). Her first chapbook is *One Bare Foot* (Zeitgeist Press, 2018), and her second is forthcoming from Finishing Line Press in fall 2022.

Ed Ruzicka knocked around the country and globe a bit before settling in Baton Rouge, Louisiana, where he lives with his wife, Renee. Ed has two books. The most recent, *My Life in Cars*, addresses the marriage between desire and the American highway. Ed has been published in many journals and anthologies. He is an occupational therapist. More at edrpoet. com.

Karen Sadler (she/her) is a geriatric millennial living in Toronto with her husband and two young kids. She writes about grief, nature, parenthood, and the occasional ghost. You can find more of her writing on Instagram at @kallorywrites.

Kristine Scarrow (she/her) is the author of four young adult novels and spent the last five years as a hospital writer in residence. She is in her final year of the MFA in writing program at the University of Saskatchewan. She is working on a short story collection and lives in Saskatoon.

Ali Sharman (she/her) lives in the northwest of England with her husband, two sons, and fluffy dog. She is an English teacher and former journalist, but her real passion is writing poetry and fiction.

Betsy Sharp (she/her) works with words and clay on a small off-grid island in the Pacific Northwest. Her work has appeared in *Creative Nonfiction, The Sun, Quiddity, Crab Creek Review*, and other places.

Barbara Simmons grew up in Boston and now resides in California. The coasts inform her poetry. A graduate of Wellesley College, she received an MA in The Writing Seminars from Johns Hopkins and an MA in education and counseling from Santa Clara University. A retired educator, she continues to savor life and language, exploring words as ways to remember, envision, celebrate, mourn, and try to understand more. Publications have included *Santa Clara Review, Hartskill Review, Boston Accent, New Verse News, Soul-Lit, 300 Days of Sun, Capsule Stories, Journal of Expressive Writing, Second Chance Lit, Ekphrastic Review,* and *Writing It Real* anthologies. Her first volume of poetry, *Offertories: Exclamations and Disequilibriums,* was published in 2022.

Editorial Staff

Natasha Lioe, Founder and Publisher

Natasha Lioe graduated with a BA in narrative studies from University of Southern California. She's always had an affinity for words and stories and emotions. Her work has appeared in *Adsum Literary Magazine*, and she won the Edward B. Moses Creative Writing Competition in 2016. Her greatest strength is finding and focusing the pathos in an otherwise cold world, and she hopes to help humans tell their unique, compelling stories.

Carolina VonKampen, Publisher and Editor in Chief

Carolina VonKampen graduated with a BA in English and history and completed the University of Chicago's editing certificate program. She is available for hire as a freelance copyeditor and book designer. For more information on her freelance work, visit carolinavonkampen.com. Her writing has appeared in *So to Speak*'s blog, *FIVE:2:ONE*'s #thesideshow, *Moonchild Magazine*, and *Déraciné Magazine*. Her short story "Logan Paul Is Dead" was nominated by *Dream Pop Journal* for the 2018 Best of the Net. She tweets about editing at @carolinamarie_v and talks about books she's reading on Instagram at @carolinamariereads.

BEE LB, Reader

BEE LB is an array of letters, bound to impulse; they are a writer creating delicate connections. they have called any number of places home; currently, a single yellow wall in Michigan. they are currently working on two poetry manuscripts, *HEART GROTESQUE* and *SWALLOW THE TRUTH, COUGH UP BOTH HALVES*. they have been published in *Revolute Lit*, *Red Weather*, *opia*, *Capsule Stories*, *Catchwater Magazine*, and *Ample Remains*, among others. they joined *Capsule Stories* as a reader in January 2022. their portfolio can be found at twinbrights.carrd.co.

Aimee Brooks, Reader

Aimee Brooks is a writer, artist, and coffee lover living in West Texas. After completing an undergrad degree in ceramics, sculpture, and jewelry making, she set sail on a writing journey for personal development and has since found herself completely enamored with the written word. She is working toward acceptance to an MFA program where she can further hone her fiction skills. When she's not writing, you can find her working on graphic design projects for her job, hanging out with her husband and cat, or going to the gym with friends. You can find more of Aimee's work in *Goats Milk Magazine*, *Embers* literary magazine, and The Storytelling Project.

Stephanie Coley, Reader

Stephanie Coley is a country girl from Gering, Nebraska. She graduated in 2016 from Concordia University, Nebraska with a BA in English and a minor in art. She has been a journalism teacher, janitor, data technician, and more. Stephanie is a published poet, appearing in the National Creativity Series of 2009 and *Mango* Issue 3, Respeto, in 2017. She is also a winner of the 2020 Historic Posters Reimagined Project, which can be found at the Nebraska History Museum in Lincoln, Nebraska. Stephanie currently works as the program manager at the West Nebraska Arts Center in Scottsbluff, Nebraska. Stephanie joined *Capsule Stories* as a reader in January 2021.

Rhea Dhanbhoora, Reader

Rhea Dhanbhoora worked for close to a decade as an editor and writer before quitting her job and moving to New York to get her master's degree and finally writing the stories everyone told her no one would ever read. Her debut poetry collection, *Sandalwood-Scented Skeletons*, was published by

---

Finishing Line Press in 2022. Her work has appeared or is forthcoming in publications such as *Sparkle & Blink*, *Awakened Voices*, *Five on the Fifth*, *Capsule Stories Autumn 2020 Edition*, *Fly on the Wall Press*, *HerStry*, *Artsy*, *Broccoli Mag*, and *JMWW*. Her work has been nominated for a Pushcart Prize and Best American Essays. She is currently on the board of directors for the literary organization Quiet Lightning and editor of RealBrownTalk. Rhea joined *Capsule Stories* as a reader in January 2021. She's working on several projects, including a linked story collection about women based in the underrepresented Parsi Zoroastrian diaspora. You can read her work online at rheadhanbhoora.com.

Hannah Fortna, Reader

Hannah Fortna graduated in 2016 from Concordia University, Nebraska, combining her passion for the written word and her affinity for art making with a degree in English and a minor in photography. After a three-year career as a freelance copyeditor, she heard traveling calling her name and now works seasonal jobs in places connected to America's national parks. When she's not selling souvenirs to tourists in gift shops, she enjoys hiking, photographing natural spaces, and writing about the flora and fauna she saw while on the trail. She reads anything from poetry to middle-grade novels, but the nature-inspired creative nonfiction section is her haunt in any bookstore. Her poetry has previously appeared in *Moonchild Magazine* and *Capsule Stories Spring 2019 Edition*. Hannah joined *Capsule Stories* as a reader in November 2020.

Teya Hollier, Reader

Teya Hollier is a graduate of York University with a BA in creative writing. At York, she won both the Babs Burggraf

Award and the Judith Eve Gewurtz award for her poetry and prose. Her work has previously appeared in *Room* magazine, *Verses Magazine*, *OyeDrum Magazine*, and *Capsule Stories Second Isolation Edition*, where she was nominated for a Pushcart Prize. Teya joined *Capsule Stories* as a reader in January 2022. When she is not writing, she is reading and reviewing books, watching horror movies, drinking copious amounts of tea, and bingeing *The Great British Bake Off*. She is currently working on a collection of short stories and a ghostly novella.

Mel Lake, Reader

Mel (Melodie) Lake is a writer and editor who lives in Denver with her partner and a very good dog. She received an English BA from Northern Arizona University and an MS in technical communication from Northeastern University. Her essays have been published in *The Mark Literary Review* and *Capsule Stories* and her fiction in various places including *Stratum Press* and *Land beyond the World*. The full list of her publications can be found at mel-lake.com. She's working on a novel, is a comics nerd, and always forgets to tweet at @melofsometrades. Mel joined *Capsule Stories* as a reader in January 2022.

Kendra Nuttall, Reader

Kendra Nuttall is a copywriter by day and poet by night. She has a BA in English with an emphasis in creative writing from Utah Valley University. Her work has previously appeared in *Spectrum*, *Capsule Stories*, *Chiron Review*, and *What Rough Beast*, as well as various other journals and anthologies. She is the author of the poetry collection *A Statistical Study of Randomness* (Finishing Line Press, 2021) and *Our Bones Ache Together* (FlowerSong Press, forthcoming). Kendra lives in Utah with her husband and poodle. When she's not writing, you can find her hiking, watching reality TV, or attempting to pet every animal she sees. You can find out more about her work at kendranuttall.com. Kendra joined *Capsule Stories* as a reader in January 2021.

Rachel Skelton, Reader

Rachel Skelton graduated from William Woods University with a BA in English, a concentration in writing, and a secondary major in business administration, a concentration in management. She has interned for Dzanc Books and now works as a freelance fiction editor specializing in speculative fiction. You can find more information about her work at theeditingskeleton.com. She occasionally tweets about editing at @EditingSkeleton and talks about books she's reading at @TheReadingSkeleton on Instagram. When she's not doing anything reading-related, she's hanging out with her cats, collecting houseplants, and attempting to learn how to crochet. Rachel joined *Capsule Stories* as a reader in January 2021.

Deanne Sleet, Reader

Deanne Sleet is a graduate of Saint Louis University with a BA in English, a concentration in creative writing, and minors in African American studies and women's and gender studies. She has interned for *River Styx* and Midwest Artist Project Services, where she gained experience with grant writing, editing, and writing copy. She is currently the leasing and marketing manager at City Lofts on Laclede and holds the secretary position for SLU's Black Alumni Association. She writes short fiction and poetry, and a novel is in the making. In her spare time, she hangs out with her cat and roller-skates. Deanne joined *Capsule Stories* as a reader in February 2021.

Annie Powell Stone, Reader

Annie Powell Stone (she/her) is a fan of peanut butter toast. Poetry recently came back to her after many years away and has absolutely saved her sanity during lockdown. Her work has appeared in *Door Is a Jar*, among others. Her published poetry can be found in her online portfolio at https://5fd9df8032a50.site123.me/. She joined *Capsule Stories* as a reader in March 2022. Annie got her BA in English from the University of Maryland and her MS in education from the University of Pennsylvania. She is currently pursuing accreditation from the Orton-Gillingham Academy for her work as a reading specialist with kids. She lives on the ancestral land of the Piscataway people with her husband and two kiddos in Baltimore City, Maryland, where she proudly holds the post of Front Desk Lady at a small K–8 school. Read more of her poetry on Instagram at @anniepowellstone.

Claire Taylor, Reader

Claire Taylor is a writer in Baltimore, Maryland, where she lives with her husband, son, a bossy old cat, and an anxious dog who longs to be the cat's best friend. Claire's writing has appeared in a variety of publications, and she was a finalist for the 2020 Lascaux Prize in Poetry and winner of the 2021 *Serotonin* New Year's Day poetry competition. Her micro-chapbook, *A History of Rats*, is available from Ghost City Press. Claire is the founder and editor in chief of *Little Thoughts Press*, a print literary magazine of writing for and by kids. Claire joined *Capsule Stories* as a reader in March 2021. A selection of Claire's work is available online at clairemtaylor.com.

Emily Uduwana, Reader

Emily Uduwana (she/her) is a poet and short fiction author based in California. She received her BA in history from CSU Northridge and her MA in history from UC Riverside, where she focused on queerness, gender, and sexuality in early California. Her work can be found on her website and in publications like *FUNGI Magazine*, *Stonecoast Review*, and *Capsule Stories Autumn 2021 Edition*. Her debut poetry chapbooks, *Knotted* and *An Expedition to the Desert of Andromeda*, were released in 2020 by orangeapplepress and Roaring Junior Press. Her next chapbook and first collection are forthcoming from Louisiana Literature Press and Nightingale & Sparrow Press in 2022. Emily joined *Capsule Stories* as a reader in January 2022.

Amy Wang, Reader

Amy Wang is a student from California. Her work has been recognized by the Scholastic Art and Writing Awards, the YoungArts Foundation, and Columbia College Chicago, among others. In her free time, you can find her crying over fanfiction or translating Chinese literature. Amy joined *Capsule Stories* as a reader in January 2022.

Submission Guidelines

Capsule Stories **is a print literary magazine** published once every season. Our first issue was published on March 1, 2019, and we accept submissions year-round.

Become published in a literary magazine run by like-minded people. We have a penchant for pretty words, an affinity to the melancholy, and an undeniably time-ful aura. We believe that stories exist in a specific moment, and that that moment is what makes those stories unique.

What we're really looking for are stories that can touch the heart. Stories that come from the heart. Stories about love, identity, the self, the world, the human condition. Stories that show what living in this world as the human you are is like.

We accept short stories, poems, and remarkably written essays. For short stories and essays, we're interested in pieces under 3,000 words. You may include up to five poems in a single poetry submission (please send them all in one Word document), and only send one story or essay at a time. Please send previously unpublished work only ("published" includes pieces that have been posted or made publicly available on a blog, website, or social media platform). You may only submit one submission per edition. Simultaneous submissions are okay, but please let us know if your submission is accepted elsewhere. Please include a brief third-person bio with your submission, and attach your submissions in a Word document (no PDFs unless your poetry has very specific formatting, please!).

Find our full submission guidelines and current theme descriptions at capsulestories.com/submissions.

Connect with us!
capsulestories.com
@CapsuleStories on Twitter and Facebook
@CapsuleStoriesMag on Instagram